I0771430

To anyone who has ever walked into a space and wondered: Do I belong here?
To anyone who has doubted themselves and thought: Am I capable of doing this?
To anyone who looked at themselves in the mirror and pondered: Am I good enough?

You do.
You are.
You are better than enough.
And this book is for you.

Spellbound beneath Sapphire Skies

AMBER LEIGH LARRAIN

A.L.L. BOOKS
EST 2024

BEFORE IT ALL BEGAN...

Willow sat in her small studio apartment, sifting through the large pile of mail. Each week the letters grew a deeper shade of red as she got further away from her last unemployment check. Just looking at the unwelcoming pile made anxiety rattle within her. She tossed the red envelopes to the side to sift through junk mail instead. One letter, a deep sapphire envelope with golden writing, caught her attention. This seemed more inviting than opening bills she couldn't afford to pay, so she quickly opened it. Inside was cream-colored parchment with familiar loopy writing.

My dearest Willow,
Thank you from the bottom of my heart for taking care of me in my final days. By the time you get this letter, I will have moved on beyond the glittering veil, to greener pastures, to the big guy in the sky, yada yada.

My last request of you, my dear girl, is to take care of my bookshop until it can be sold. It should be only two weeks. Please use the enclosed check as payment for your two weeks' work at the shop.

There is a small apartment above the shop that you can live in while you are there. Though it will be a big change from the city, I think you'll find it a welcoming and lovely place to spend some time.

A car will come to pick you up tomorrow morning at 9am sharp.

All my love,

Aunt Tilly

WILLOW LET OUT A DEEP SIGH. THE FINAL DAYS WITH HER aunt had been difficult as Willow watched her slowly fade away like sand through one's fingers. With each passing day after, she had prepared herself for this news. No matter how much you try to mentally prepare for this though, nothing can take away the pain of knowing you'll never be able to pick up the phone and hear their voice, or see that look on their face —the one that says, "I'm glad you are here."

She reread the letter but none of it made sense. She feared her aunt must have been delusional in her final days. Willow was sure she never owned a bookshop. Not once in her 32 years did she mention it. Willow peered inside the envelope where she did find a check, with a very, *very* large sum written on it. Her blue eyes widened in surprise. Something between a gasp and a cry slipped from her lips. She couldn't possibly cash this check. However, if she did she would be able to pay her bills for half a year.

. . .

THE NEXT MORNING, WILLOW AWOKE TO THE SOUND OF WHAT was apparently a car horn, which wouldn't be out of the ordinary in New York City, except instead of blaring it chimed like soft bells. It was what she imagined falling glitter would sound like if it were audible. She pulled back the green velvet curtains and peered out her window. There was a car parking right in front of her building. Where traffic in New York City moved like an angry bull, this car pulled up like a gentle breeze.

Willow bounded down the steps fully intending to tell the driver that there was no way she was able to leave her life here to work at some random bookshop—she didn't even like reading!

When she knocked on the car door it was empty, but there was another sapphire card lying on the backseat with her name written in gold. Willow got in to look at the letter, and the door shut and locked behind her. "Let me out!" she started to scream as she beat her palm against the window. Then she noticed the card rise from her lap. Willow stopped pounding and turned her attention to the levitating card. It turned itself around, opened the flap, and out floated the letter. It gracefully landed in her lap like a leaf falling from its branch as the car started to speed out of the city. The shock of seeing this caused her to momentarily forget the danger she might be in, fear replaced by curiosity and amazement.

My dearest Willow,

Thank you for agreeing to take over the bookshop. This car will take you right to the front door of the store. Your apartment sits directly above it.

I hope you will find it a wonderful place to both work and live for the next two weeks.

Once there, you will have the day to get acquainted with the shop. It is my hope that you will reopen the next day. Your new town depends on this shop so please don't take more than a day to get acquainted.

Remember, it is only fourteen days! It will go by before you know it.

All My Love,
Aunt Tilly

"One day! I don't even know if I can name more than a book or two, and I'm supposed to set up an entire bookshop in a day! And she's practically kidnapped me!" she said aloud to herself. Then she looked down at the letter as words began to appear one by one as if they were being written by an unseen hand.

P.S. Surely you know more than two books! I've given you a book each birthday for years. You read them… Didn't you?

P.P.S. It's not kidnapping! You are a full grown woman.

The city became a blur as the car continued to pick up speed. When it finally slowed, the world around her seemed to have undergone a magnificent change. Oak trees stood tall and strong with flaking bark like peeling wallpaper. Their outstretched, bendy branches lined the dirt covered roads, creating a woven canopy overhead. Spanish moss lay lazily around some branches, hanging down so effortlessly. It felt as if she had been placed into an impressionist painting.

Through the leaves she could see glimpses of sky. It had cerulean clouds and was the deepest blue she had ever seen. She picked up the letter and whispered, "Where are we?" But no additional messages appeared. She shook the letter. "Tilly, where are we? You better not have taken me to New Jersey!"

Though she doubted she could run a bookshop, a jarring thought occurred to her. Would anyone even notice she was gone? Her last family member had just passed away. The man she had been dating ghosted her recently, and she didn't have a job. Who was there to miss her? To wonder why this girl got into a strange driverless car and never returned?

The car finally came to a full stop in front of a wooden sign that simply read, "Books." Standing outside of the bookshop was what looked like a small boy, but he had the face of a middle aged man. He couldn't have been more than two feet tall. His cheeks were red and puffy. The man looked just like one of those garden gnomes she saw on people's front lawns whenever she made it out to the suburbs. He was dressed in a fine suit with a sash that read, "Mayor." Atop his head was a red felt pointy hat. His long white beard was the color of newly fallen snow and looked just as soft. Surprisingly, his voice was deep like a drum beat, and Willow flinched a bit from surprise.

"Welcome, Willow!"

Out of habit, she tucked her short auburn hair behind her ears. Willow looked around as if she were checking for other nearby Willows. As there were none, she crouched down and extended her hand to the man.

He continued, "First, I want to say that I'm so sorry for the passing of your aunt. She has run this bookshop for the past 300 years."

Willow choked. "I'm sorry, what did you say?"

He repeated himself loudly this time assuming she must have a hearing problem. Willow decided her grief must be driving her mad.

The mayor pointed to the wooden sign hanging above the entrance. "This is your aunt's bookshop. Was—now it is yours for the time being."

"Two weeks," she interjected.

"Yes, that's right. Anyway, if you prefer to rename the shop to your liking, just tell it so and it will change."

Willow shook her head, not comprehending, "I'm sorry—tell who?"

The mayor furrowed his brow and looked at her curiously. "The sign. Tell the sign."

"Oh yes. Of course!" she said brightly, pretending to understand what he meant, and he smiled back at her.

The mayor then handed her a large brass key. "I'll let you get to it."

"Yes, I'll get to it!" she said, using the "fake it until you make it" enthusiasm her latest self-help book had encouraged, but when she looked back at the mayor to ask a question, he was already gone.

Willow opened the bookshop and was instantly overwhelmed by the size of it. From the outside it looked like a tiny cottage with white stucco walls and a thatched roof—something you might see on a postcard from the English countryside. It immediately made her want a cup of tea.

Once inside, however, it was rather large and home to thousands of books. She took a deep inhale. Each room was its own genre, and it seemed like each room led to another, endlessly. It occurred to her that she didn't even know how to get back to the beginning. And so much like in life, she wandered aimlessly until she found where she needed to be.

Self-doubt began to wash over her. She hadn't been able to keep a job for more than a year her whole life—how could she possibly be successful in something she had no interest in and no knowledge about?

Willow pulled out her cellphone and texted her boyfriend, if he could even be called that at this point. He had stopped answering her texts weeks ago.

> I'm going to be gone for two weeks. My aunt passed away and I need to take care of her affairs.

She waited several minutes before he responded.

> K. Sorry about your aunt.

Willow's eyes rolled as she shook her head.

> When I get back, I don't think we should see each other again.

The only reply came several minutes later when he gave her last text a "thumbs up".

Jamming the phone's side buttons, she powered it down and tossed it under the counter. This would be a good time to disconnect from the phone, she thought to herself. The word *disconnect* played in her head over and over as it changed shape and took on its own life. She had thought she was in control of it, as if she were choosing to disconnect from everything around her, but as she struggled with the word, it taunted her. She realized that *she was disconnected*…from others, from her life, from feeling like things mattered. And as the thoughts grew, they became crueler—intending to wound her: *You are disconnected because no one wants to connect with you. And you have no way to reconnect, to be valued, to matter.*

Her breathing became erratic as she tried to quash the

voice. She pulled out a worry rock from her pocket. A deep groove down the center, a visual of how strongly she needed stability. She pressed deeper and deeper, until the voice was low but still hovering. With the rock still in hand, she wandered the shop some more.

SHE HADN'T A CLUE WHERE TO BEGIN OR WHAT NEEDED TO BE done. No directions had been provided. She continued to walk around the twisty bookshop for hours, trying to learn what categories of books were carried and where to find them. "Who knew hockey romance was its own genre? Not I," she thought to herself. Willow saw a cover that caught her eye only because the spine was her favorite color of royal purple. She slipped it into the large pocket of her old cardigan. Maybe this would start her love of reading—stranger things have happened.

As she looked around, she felt lost, lost within the books, lost within herself. She really couldn't handle another failure. Each failure had been a pitstop on the roadmap that got her to this point. Now when she tried something new, she failed intentionally so she could say to herself, "I did this!" Failure had become the one thing she could succeed at accomplishing.

The room began to spin, and closing her eyes didn't cease the sensation. She sank down to the floor, gripping the shelf to steady herself, because even on the floor she felt as if she might fall over. Her breath began to take over her whole body as she heaved air that was violently pulled in and out of her chest beyond her control. Her hands began to tremble and she closed her eyes again to try to focus on calming herself down. When her body finally yielded to the panic, waved a white flag in defeat, it regulated itself. The calm was no relief, though, as she was completely exhausted.

She carefully climbed the steps to the apartment, clutching

the handrail to steady her weary body. She unlocked the door and inside were all of her belongings just as she had them arranged back in New York City. Her green loveseat that she had bought at a used furniture shop. The black coffee table someone had put out with the trash, that she rescued from a life at the landfill. And on the wooden end table was a photo of her and her mother.

"What a strange place," she thought. Willow took out the romance novel that was still in her cardigan pocket and tossed it onto her coffee table. She sank carefully onto the couch, trying to be gentle with herself. Then she threw her mustard yellow knitted blanket over herself, blocking out the world. The panic attack had subsided but it had zapped every ounce of energy from her. Willow closed her eyes and was asleep within minutes. She didn't wake until the next day.

DAY 1

A hummingbird appeared at the window, alerting her to start her day. At first she was in awe of the beautiful bird. She had seen a hummingbird once or twice before but they always quickly darted off. This one lingered and she was able to examine all the little details, watching its petite iridescent wings morph from pinks to blues to purples.

Then reality smacked her in the face—she had gone to bed so early last night and lost her entire day to prepare the bookshop! "Oh no, oh no, oh no!" She cupped her hands around her face, realizing she had screwed up yet again.

To everyone around her, she looked like a normal, happy, healthy woman. But inside, she doubted everything she said and did. The silent yet nagging feeling like she was never good enough for any space she existed in.

And here she was, being given another opportunity to fail. She couldn't understand why her aunt, knowing how much she struggled to just keep putting one foot in front of the other, knowing how difficult it was to say, "just wake up for one more day," *every single day*, would put her in this wholly unfamiliar situation! One she was certain to flounder in! Though she loved her deeply, she felt a twinge of resentment.

As those thoughts ran through her mind, she watched the rays of sunlight dance on the wooden floor—another reminder that it was time to leave the apartment and start her day. Willow got out of bed and got dressed for her first day as a bookstore owner, albeit quite a temporary one. Though she felt totally out of her element, she did prefer that title over "unemployed spinster."

"You can do this," she whispered to herself, applying the "self-talk" tactic she had learned from another self-help book. Then she put one foot in front of the other and got ready to leave. "It's just two weeks. You can do anything for two weeks!" she said, trying to pump herself up. Then the little voice said, "You didn't make it two weeks at the law firm." She wished she could tell that little voice in her head to take a hike, but she knew there was no getting it to go away.

When she opened the door to the small apartment that led to the bookshop below, the smell of sugar and cinnamon wafted through the air. She eagerly followed the sweet scent in hopes of finding a treat to start her day.

There was a small cafe off to the side with a gray stone fireplace. Just in front of it was a children's section. She realized she'd have to learn more than just familiarizing herself with the layout and book titles—she'd have to learn to make coffee, pastries, understand the financial aspects of running a business, and how to run a children's story hour. What if there were other things she needed to do that she hadn't even thought of yet? It all seemed impossible to figure out without a mentor. Willow felt a pang of grief; she wished her aunt were here to guide her.

In the small cafe section was a man with brown hair swept across his forehead and a strong jaw. She watched as he was pulling sweet cinnamon rolls out of the oven. As she approached, she noticed that in fact he was not a man, but a centaur. Willow blinked her eyes rapidly, convinced she was seeing things. But just from the way he held himself she could admire his elegance and confidence. She felt a little envious of it. It made her adjust her own posture and stand a bit straighter.

"Good morning to you, Ms.… Well actually I don't think Ms. Tilly told me your name," he said warmly.

"I'm her niece, Willow," she said, and started to stick out her hand for a shake but quickly withdrew it. She second guessed herself. With four hooves and two arms, she wasn't sure what the standard greeting for a centaur would be.

The centaur laughed good-naturedly. "You're fine. Are you ready for your first day?"

"Honestly, no. I'm actually not sure why I'm here. Between me and you, I don't even like to read."

"Hmmm. Maybe you haven't found the right book. Anyway, would you like to taste one of the cinnamon rolls? I made them out of habit but forgot that I should probably clear the menu with you."

"I never met a cinnamon roll I didn't like. However, I think tasting this, just to be sure, is a very good first action to take as the town's substitute bookseller."

A small white plate with purple flowers around the edges was placed in front of her. The roll was so fresh that steam twirled above it and warm white icing flowed down the sides. She took one bite and the cinnamon roll melted in her mouth. A sound of sheer approval followed. "I take it you like it?" he said.

"I've never tasted anything so amazing in my life! I think I'll eat this for breakfast, lunch, and dinner!"

He laughed again and she noted that she liked the sound of his laughter very much. It made her feel welcome here and she recognized how much she needed that.

"I didn't catch your name," she said and then shoved another large bite into her mouth.

"Daylin. I've been working here for about five years."

"And I hope you will work here another 500!" She meant

it as a joke and hoped she'd hear the sound of his deep laughter again.

Instead he replied seriously, "I probably will. Not sure anyone else in town is much of a baker. Anyway, I consider this my second home."

After Willow devoured the cinnamon bun, she scraped the fork along the plate to get the last bits of icing, but resisted the urge to lick the plate clean. She then followed it up with a warm caramel latte that she drank slowly, taking her time—as to savor it, she told herself, but in the back of her mind she knew she was delaying the daunting task of starting her work day.

Her hands were cupped around the mug, absorbing its warmth. She and Daylin spoke easily the whole time. Her list of questions about the shop was endless and she was able to gain a few answers before she finished her drink.

Once her plate and cup were empty she decided to excuse herself. "Well, I guess I'll go and…do book stuff."

He laughed again and said, "I wish you much success in… book stuff."

She couldn't help but smile back at him.

Willow went to the large oak front counter to wait for her first customer. She wasn't sure what to do so she began to clean the counter with a paper towel, despite the fact that it was already perfectly clean. Then she looked around, wondering what she should do next.

A woman with fierce purple hair and a dress to match walked in. Willow adjusted her cardigan as she panicked at the thought of her first customer! She thought about how she'd greet the customer, "Welcome to…Books." No, she thought, that sounded ridiculous.

By the time she settled on a greeting, the woman had walked past her and sat on the couch.

"Good morning! How can I help—"

"I'm good. Thanks."

"Ok, well I'll be at the counter when you need me."

Willow kept looking her way, waiting for her to ask for help or to get up to peruse the books. However, she just sat and looked through the book she brought.

Just then, a group of teenage wizards came bounding in. Willow froze for a moment, worried she wouldn't be able to find their books or know how to ring them up.

"Hello! May I help you?"

"Nah, we're good."

Her muscles relaxed a bit. The oldest of the bunch lifted his wand and a stack of books flew to him. He repeated this until each child had their own stack of books. Willow watched on in amazement. They handed over their money and left with their school books. She wondered if all the customers would be this easy to help or if she was even needed here at all.

It was several hours before the next customer entered. It was another teen wizard but this one was alone. He came in, eyes darting around the shop, dragging his broom by his side.

"Hello! May I help you?" she asked again, hoping he could also find his way.

He hung his head, "I need school books, but someone tossed my bookbag in the lake. I haven't learned the spell to retrieve it. Ironically, the spellbook with the drying spell now sits at the bottom of the lake." He sighed wearily, "Have you got the list of what is needed for middle years?"

Willow didn't even know what middle years meant and she certainly didn't know what books they needed. "Well, I think I can help you find what you need," Willow said, knowing this was entirely false.

The woman with the purple hair made eye contact. Her eyes were the color of lavender fields and Willow would have continued to stare if the woman's actions hadn't snapped her out of it. She took her wand and tapped the floor. A glowing path appeared on the floor, and Willow followed the shimmering golden light with the boy in tow. He was still dragging his broom and it sounded like little mice scurrying across the floor. When they got to the textbook section, the books rattled on the shelves and Willow grabbed them one by one. Then she handed them to the boy.

Sheer amazement overtook her face. She turned around to the boy, eager to ask, "Have you ever seen anything so amazing in your life?"

But he looked on unimpressed and simply said, "Thanks."

Willow felt there was something about this boy that felt familiar. She couldn't place what it was. As they followed the line back to the front, she tried to make conversation with him.

"So what's your name?"

"Santiv."

"And you go to school with the other wizards?"

"Yeah, unfortunately," Santiv mumbled. "They are the ones who tossed my backpack into the water."

"I'm so sorry." Willow wasn't sure what else to say or ask him so they continued on in silence, all the while her mind pondering what she felt was so familiar about him.

By the time she got to the front, the woman who had helped her was gone. She wished she had the chance to thank her.

When her day was done, she went to the cafe to wish Daylin a good evening. He handed her a plate.

"Hope you had a good first day, Boss," he said.

"I did. Thanks."

"I wasn't sure if you had time to get food yet, so I made you dinner."

A wave of warmth washed over her. It felt good to be taken care of for a change.

She eagerly went up to the quiet of her apartment, plate in hand. The day hadn't started off strong, but overall it went well enough for someone who had no idea what she was doing. After eating the delicious meal of baked chicken and mashed potatoes, she walked to the calendar and marked a large "X" over the day. "Only 13 more days to go," she thought to herself.

Silence enveloped her. The stillness and quiet of the night was unsettling. For years, the sound of traffic and people chattering as they moved on the sidewalk below had lulled her to sleep. Last night the exhaustion from her panic attack had not given her the time to notice how painfully silent it was. How could she possibly sleep like this?

Willow tried grabbing the romance novel she had put on the table yesterday. She attempted to read it, but it just didn't catch her attention. Her eyes would move over the words, unthinking, much like a driver on a long commute. After four or five pages, she couldn't even recall what she had read so she tossed the book back on the table.

With so much quiet, her mind wandered. She thought of all the things back home that she did miss: her local pastry shop, the neighbor's cat down the hall that often stopped by, the bustling crowds of people that she had no connection to but felt a comfort from their presence. And as she thought of her home, she closed her eyes and could almost hear the cars and the people, and finally sleep came to her.

DAY 2

The clock chimed softly nine times and Willow walked to the front door to flip the wooden sign from "Closed" to "Open". She felt small fireworks in her stomach. A few minutes later, the same woman who had been so helpful yesterday walked in. Though she was dressed in a different outfit, it was still all purple and coordinated with her hair. Today it was in a messy bun atop her head and resembled a flower ready to bloom. Willow felt so dressed down in her oversized cardigan and jean skirt.

The purple-haired woman sat on one of the large, worn couches. It formed around her body as she sank into the cushion. Like yesterday, she went right to working in a notebook. Willow thought the woman was about her age, but was also quickly learning she wasn't good at assessing people's ages here.

"How odd," Willow thought. "She isn't even going to pretend to shop." But before she could comment, three little girls bounded in. Each looked exactly alike, and they were dressed in the same dress and bows, though each had their own color.

"Hello," chimed the first girl dressed all in red.

"We are the Sapphire Forest welcome crew," said the second girl, who was in all green. Then they all erupted into a fit of giggles.

"Hello. I'm Willow…the very temporary owner of this bookshop," trying to hide the nervousness in her voice.

"Our father is the Mayor. Does that mean we get free books?" said the last little girl, all dressed in white.

Willow had no idea how to respond and looked up at the woman sitting on the couch. She ever so slightly shook her head no. "I'm afraid not," Willow told them.

Then, she noticed that each girl had a small grey or black butterfly above their shoulder. "How interesting," Willow started to say as she pointed to one of their shoulders. A loud cough emitted from the woman on the couch. When Willow looked up at her she vigorously shook her head. Willow awkwardly moved her hand in a sweeping motion towards the cafe. "How interesting that I have three cookies that are just waiting to be eaten by three charming young ladies. Do you know of any such ladies?" Their smiles reached their ears as they dashed off to the cafe area to claim their sweets.

As the girls were happily munching away, Willow approached the woman on the couch.

"Thank you for your help. I'm Willow, Tilly's niece."

"Hello, I'm Faeble."

"Like a story?"

"Exactly."

"Why did you discourage me from asking about the butterflies? I've never seen butterflies that are trained as pets like that before," Willow asked with genuine curiosity.

"They aren't pets. Butterflies can't be trained."

"Oh yes, of course," said Willow, feeling self-conscious about how little she understood here.

"They are guardians of sorts. The girls' mother passed away a few months back. The butterflies are their grief guardians, which is why their shades vary, from girl to girl, from time to time. When their hearts heal as best they can, the butterflies will transform into their destined colors and they will set themselves free, but will always remain nearby."

Willow glanced over at the girls, still munching away on their cookies, little crumbs falling to the table as they did so. There was a sadness in their eyes that she noticed now, that was originally masked by their sheer excitement and energy. Willow felt her throat clench. She sat down on the couch next to the woman. "How sad. They are so little." She glanced around the shop. "I wonder if there are any books here that could help them with their healing process. I'm afraid I haven't had much time to learn the entire collection we have."

"I'm sure you will find something just right, when they are ready for it," Faeble said with a smile.

"I'm curious. Why a butterfly?"

"Why not?"

"Well you have no shortage of magical creatures here."

Faeble nodded. "Butterflies are like one's grief in many ways. It's ever-changing. It can feel like you are encased in it at first, as if nothing else in the world can be seen, heard, or felt. And then some day, it is lighter but still there, ebbing and flowing with good days and bad days, like a butterfly's movements in a flower field."

Willow sat with that for a moment before responding. "That makes perfect sense actually."

Then without another word, Faeble went back to her tan leather-bound journal.

Willow looked up to see the three girls skipping out of the shop. "One group of customers successfully handled," she thought to herself. Despite this small victory, the nagging feeling that she was going to fail kept creeping into her thoughts like an invasive vine.

The next customer didn't come in until after lunch. A wave of cold air swept through the shop as he moved closer to her. Willow shivered from the sudden drop in temperature. In his arms he held a stack of books and plopped them on the table.

"I'd like to return these," he said in a gruff voice. He was easily over six feet tall and covered in white hair. His eyes were blue as glacial ice.

Willow tried to hide surprise from her face. "Was there something wrong with the books?" Though she tried to calm herself, the sheer size of this disgruntled man made her palms sweaty and her voice quiver.

He averted her gaze. "No…" he admitted. She took note of the bent spines but was too afraid to say anything.

Then Faeble, as she seemed to have a habit of doing, chimed in. "Did you happen to read those books?"

The man grunted.

"You know you can't return books you've read, Heilo."

Without another word, he picked up the books and left the store, muttering under his breath.

This was the third time Faeble had come to her rescue, and it was only her second day here. Willow was curious about this woman who seemed like she'd pass the whole day in the shop but not spend a penny. The New Yorker in her wanted to sarcastically quip that "this isn't a library, ya know?" But she held back, appreciating the woman's help in navigating three situations she didn't know how to handle on her own.

"I have no idea what I am doing here," Willow admitted to Faeble. "I didn't even know the return policy."

"You are here to help out your aunt and that is exactly what you are doing right now. If you weren't here, the shop would be closed. You'll figure all the rest out," she replied kindly.

"I'm kinda notorious for not figuring things out."

"I do not think you are notorious for this. Is your inability to figure things out known on a global scale?"

Willow chuckled, though Faeble just waited for a response. "No, luckily it hasn't gotten to that point…yet."

"Well then there is still time to turn it around. To look at this new adventure and say, 'This time I will do it well. I will not fail,' and then follow through with that mindset until it is true and works out as such."

"I'm only here for two weeks."

"Even better. Surely you can't bankrupt the entire book-shop in two weeks, given it is the only bookshop in town."

Willow considered this for a second and was about to respond, but then Faeble turned back to her journal. Willow wondered why this woman was so willing to help each time but so very closed-off otherwise. How she had such wise words to share, but nothing else.

After years of struggling, Willow had listened to nearly every self-help book possible. So much so that some of the information started to contradict previous things she had learned and implemented. Should she force herself to try new things? Or lean into the things she knew she was good at? Should she turn inward and focus on her own healing? Or go out and make friends who can help her on that journey?

She wandered the corridors of books, looking for the self-help section. Maybe she'd find something new, something to pull her out of this slump. She was always looking, always searching. After working herself through the maze of books and out again to the other side, she landed right back where she had started.

Daylin was in the kitchen, preparing a fresh salad.

"Hey, Daylin. I'm curious as to where I'd find the self-help books. Not for me of course, just trying to get to know the store better."

He looked up as he lifted and tipped the large cutting board. It created a ribbon of bright red as freshly chopped strawberries fell into the bowl. "I haven't seen one. But if there is something someone needs, it may just materialize."

She was too afraid to ask any more questions, worried she might give herself away.

"Have you had time to stock up on food?" he asked.

Willow laughed, "I haven't even had a chance to leave this building yet!"

He put the salad, a rainbow of colors, onto a plate and handed it to her. With one bite, she marveled at how fresh it was and how the flavors combined perfectly as if they were always meant to be together.

He continued, "You should try to get out though. It's a lovely place to walk around."

She promised she would, though she worried she might get lost and not find her way back.

"You'll always be led to where you need to go," he said, smiling at her.

After finishing her meal, Willow wandered through the books. She peaked at each shelf, waiting to see if anything would materialize. Nothing did. She was on her own at this point.

While the sun set and darkness crept in, the bookshop slowly began to lose its vibrancy. Willow decided her workday was done, flipped the sign to "Closed," and exhaled deeply. Briefly she considered going for a walk, but felt too tired to explore and too nervous to leave the comfort of the shop. Eagerly she climbed the circular wooden staircase to her room.

She pulled back the covers over her mattress and slipped in, letting her body slowly warm the bed. The room was pitch black and silent. She tossed and turned, rolling around in the quiet just to cause some noise, some commotion. Finally, sleep came to her, and it was the best night of sleep she ever had.

DAY 3

The next morning, Willow went to her calendar and crossed off another day until she could return home. She picked out a sienna cardigan and jean miniskirt, and put on her black boots. This was her go-to outfit, comfortable and unassuming.

Then she opened the shop. Daylin was working in the cafe, creating something that filled the shop with the smell of honey. Her stomach began to growl.

"I could hear that all the way over here! Don't be shy, come try this," he said warmly.

"Well, only because I must be in charge of the cafe's quality control."

"Naturally," he said with a chuckle. His eyes seemed to sparkle when he laughed.

Placed before her was a honey latte and a small plate with a vanilla cake drizzled with golden honey on top. Willow took a bite and closed her eyes so all she could focus on was the taste. When she opened her eyes, Daylin was smiling at her.

"That bad?" And he laughed.

"Absolutely awful. You'll have to keep making me more until you get it just right," she said, winking at him. "But seriously, this tastes like my childhood," and then she paused. "That was an odd thing to say, right? Didn't make any sense."

He shook his head. "All good treats should remind you of when you were young, when things were simpler and a bit of sugar could make your whole day grand." And with his words, her embarrassment melted away like ice on a hot day.

He stayed with her while she ate and drank. She told him a little bit about her life in the city, and he told her about how he had started working here. He also shared some ideas for new desserts.

"All that sounds amazing! I'd love to come up with some ideas of my own, if that isn't stepping on your fee—hooves."

"I'm up for trying anything once," he responded.

"Thanks, Daylin," she said softly, just a touch above a whisper.

"No problem. I'm eager to learn to make new things. Expand my skills."

"No. I mean for making my transition here so easy. I know it can be difficult to suddenly have someone new to work with."

"You're a good boss, Willow," he said.

"Oh, stop. You are just buttering me up. You know I can't fire you, right?"

"I'm serious. You've handled every new situation that's come your way without shedding a single tear."

"Actually, I've shed quite a few. I just do it in hiding."

"Doesn't count if no one sees it. It's like that saying, 'if a tear falls and no one is around to notice…'"

"You've definitely got that all wrong," she said giggling.

Daylin went back to the cafe to prepare the lunch sandwiches. "You're a good boss," she repeated to herself. She had never pictured herself as someone else's boss, but with an employee as easygoing and hard-working as Daylin, she felt like she could handle it. Maybe back at home she'd apply to run a nearby cafe.

She sat at the table with her sketchbook, trying to draw up some desserts she'd love to have in the shop. She knew she only had a short time here and wanted to take advantage of having an eager pastry chef at her disposal. Once she went back to New York, she'd have to return to her local pastry shop, which was delicious but never carried her favorite desserts.

Willow put away the drawings and decided it was time to tackle the large stack of books on the counter. She picked up a few at a time. As she wandered past the fiction section, a book rattled loudly on the shelf. Willow walked away, and it stopped...then she backtracked, which sent it rattling all over again. She played this cat and mouse game several times, finding it amusing.

A customer walked by. "That book is trying to tell you something," she said over her shoulder as she selected a book.

Willow leaned close to the book but heard nothing. She looked around to make sure no one was watching her before whispering, "Hello?" to the book. No response. "Well if you aren't going to tell me, I'm going back to restocking." She shook her head, unsure if she was more upset that the book didn't respond or that she was now a person who thought books could communicate. Was she losing it?

The rest of the day was uneventful. Kind customers came and went. Willow was able to help them all.

Faeble, hearing the bells chime six, put her items into her satchel and walked out the door. Willow followed behind her.

"Hey! Um, I haven't really met anyone here yet, and I haven't even left here since I arrived. I'm going a bit stir crazy. Any suggestions on places to go?"

Faeble just walked away. Willow stood there dumbfounded and hurt. Did she not even deserve a response? But then she heard Faeble say, "Are you coming or not?" Willow picked up her pace to catch up with her. They walked for nearly half an hour in silence, watching the landscape change from a small town to a sea of beautiful trees.

"Here we are," Faeble said, turning to Willow for the first time.

"Are we hiking? I'm afraid I'm not much of a hiker." She looked down at her black Doc Martin boots.

"Something like that. This is Sapphire Forest, which shares the name of our town. Come on."

Willow hesitated to assess the terrain but then followed. They walked along a soft dirt path lined with trees that created an archway above them, blocking out the rest of the world. It was just the two of them, encased in enchanted beauty. Fireflies danced above them like little twirling stars. Each step they took created a gold imprint on the ground that slowly vanished behind them.

"Am I dreaming?" Willow asked softly as she turned to her new friend.

"Maybe…but it's all real."

"Why is the ground glowing like that?"

"It's your connection to the Earth. It's saying, 'I see you, I feel you.'"

Willow watched wide-eyed as each step created a glowing imprint. Never had the simple act of walking caused such a reaction. She was spellbound.

There is a time when you are very small and each new thing you see is magical, and everything you do is a grand adventure. She looked around the forest with that same wonder that had left her so long ago. A smile spread across her face, and she closed her eyes to focus on that peaceful feeling. There was still wonder in the world.

Willow looked up. Her eyes traced the tree branches, which stretched in a puzzle pattern, interlocking, bending. It was as if they had agreed on a compromise for where they each could grow, working together to connect but still giving each other space. The moss that hung from the branches lay there so effortlessly. It was more than beautiful. She thought for a moment of a word that could capture how it looked and how it made her feel.

"These trees are magical," Willow said with childlike wonderment.

"No," Fae replied. "These are just regular trees."

Willow stifled a laugh.

Faeble put down her satchel and removed her violet cardigan. Willow noticed small wings on her back, which grew in size once freed. She looked like a butterfly expanding its wings for the first time. Willow's eyes widened; before her was the most beautiful creature she'd ever seen.

Faeble extended a hand to her. "Fly with me?" she said.

Willow hesitated and then took her hand. The fireflies parted, making way for their flight. She immediately closed her eyes and quickly felt the sensation of being lifted off the ground. She opened her eyes just a sliver. She felt safe and comfortable, and decided to fully open her eyes and take it all in. Soon they were perched atop the trees, admiring the beauty from a new angle.

The stars above them were golden and twinkling. Gazing at the sky above, Willow traced the imaginary patterns formed by the glowing orbs. "Those stars there—they look like a heart," she said, pointing.

Faeble looked down below to where they had just been. "You can't see the stars until you free yourself of the trees."

Willow pondered this for a moment. "I feel like you are trying to say more than you are actually saying."

Faeble smiled at her. "Maybe I am. Or maybe I'm just a crazy Fae babbling about nature. Only you can decide what meaning you take from people's words."

Willow looked at her for a long while. Fae held her gaze for a few seconds, then suddenly feeling awkward, looked down at her lap.

"I'm having a feeling," said Willow.

"Hopefully it isn't indigestion," Faeble said.

"No, it's not that. That feeling when being with someone just clicks into place, and you want to stay a little longer." Faeble didn't respond but nodded her head.

Willow's own words stunned her, because quite frankly she hadn't really ever clicked with anyone outside her family. But she liked being with Faeble. She liked how matter-of-fact she was in everything she said. If she said something, you knew it was true. It felt like you were always playing a guessing game with other people, trying to decode every word, interpret every facial expression, wondering if they actually liked you or were just being polite. Willow liked how Faeble seemed to see her differently than everyone else did, and she liked how that made her feel.

"I'd like to stay longer, too," Fae whispered.

The two women smiled at each other, because they realized that while being alone had its perks, being with someone who understood you made the world seem a little bit more perfect.

DAY 4

Though Willow was still counting down the days to return home, there were small things she was starting to appreciate about this place. She enjoyed being woken up by birds chirping instead of car horns blaring, and how each morning an amazing breakfast was just a staircase away. Stretching her arms above her head, she wondered if last night had been the best dream she ever had—soaring above an enchanted forest, and with a new friend! She didn't know which was more amazing.

As she thought about it, she got ready for the day. She slipped on a green cardigan, the color of split pea soup, and a brown corduroy miniskirt. Then she slipped her feet into her familiar leather boots.

It was Sunday and she hoped to have a lazy, easy start to the day. However, some townsfolk had other ideas in mind. Apparently Sunday was their shopping day. A soft, synchronized rapping came from the door below.

When she got to the door, she saw no one out the window. She opened it and saw the three girls, each dressed alike but in different colors. Their deep black butterflies hovered just above their shoulders.

"Good morning," Willow said, still trying to rub the sleep from her eyes. As she greeted them, several other customers bustled in.

"It's story hour!" They said all at once.

As Faeble wasn't there to confirm, Willow decided she'd have to make this decision on her own. "Yes, it certainly is. Come in," she said, trying to quickly think of what to do next.

"But first," interjected Daylin from the cafe, "we must start with Story Hour Snacks."

"Of course!" The girls said in unison as they scurried toward the display case. When Willow caught his eye, she put up her hands in prayer to thank him for the time to figure out her plan.

She went to the children's section and started to look around when a rattling noise came from a nearby shelf. She turned to see a book trying to wiggle its way off the shelf. Willow went over and though it felt absurd she put out her hands for the book to jump into, which it immediately did.

The book opened itself up in her lap as she lay in a beanbag. She ran her finger across the title, *When Dragons Fly No More: A Tale of Love and Loss*. Just the sight of it made her choke up, and she thought of her own losses—her mother and her aunt. She flipped through the book quickly as she heard the girls coming her way. Willow cleared her throat and gathered herself to give the girls a grand welcome.

"Welcome to Willow's Story Hour!" The girls each fell into their own beanbag. "I'm Willow and I'm afraid I don't know your names yet."

"Pearl!"

"Ruby!"

"Jade!"

"Very nice to meet all of you."

Willow began to read the story, each page bringing the girls closer and closer. By the last page, three little gnomes had crept into her lap. She wiped away a tear.

"Why are you crying, Willow?"

"I miss my aunt very much. And, like you all, I also lost my mother. This story reminded me of how much I love them and how I always will."

"We miss our mom, too," said Ruby as the other two nodded sadly.

"Will you tell me about her?" The triplets exchanged glances, as if seeking approval.

"She made us warm chocolate chip cookies every night, and would make us these matching dresses, and she would read to us all gathered around just like this," Pearl said.

"And she would always play with us, no matter how busy she was. She always told us we were cuter than buttons, which made no sense to me. But now I miss hearing it. And she smelled like lilacs," added Jade.

Willow looked to Ruby to see if she wanted to speak. At first she shook her head but then quietly she added, "She was our mommy."

Willow looked up toward the ceiling, trying to hold in the tears that welled in her eyes. "She sounds lovely. Just lovely." Willow looked over at the gnomes to see that the butterflies were perched on each girl's shoulder, no longer hovering above it. They had turned as black as the night sky.

"Yes," they whispered in unison. For just a moment, the butterflies each flashed a bit of color, and Willow sucked in a breath as Ruby laid her head on her shoulder.

She recalled the night she lost her mother. Her mother had been a night nurse her whole life. It was a noble job, but Willow thought about how her sleeping during the day and working at night, never keeping the same schedule, drew a wedge between them. There weren't enough lazy mornings together, enough hugs. Her childhood, like all of ours, went by too quickly. Her mother had been sick for months, and two days before Willow became an adult, her mother passed in her arms.

All she could think about as she held her mother was how cruel death was. That it sucked out your personality but left the big heavy body as if mocking you. "I'm still here, I just can't talk to you." We always recognize people by their faces, but once they pass, death only takes their personality and leaves the rest of them, taunting you as to what was but no longer is.

LATER THAT DAY, WILLOW WAS AT THE COUNTER. SHE WAS trying to organize a new shipment of bookmarks and other knick-knacks that would be placed near the checkout. After she set up a display of small boxes, curiosity got the best of her and she opened one. Inside was a small plastic rainbow. She took it out and placed it on the counter, hoping to make a display to entice customers to add on to their purchases. However, once she placed the item down, it melted away.

"Oh no!" she exclaimed, worried about wasting products. A customer walking by noticed her distress and pointed above her. She looked up and the most beautiful, glowing rainbow arched above the counter. It stayed illuminated for several minutes and Willow couldn't take her eyes off of it.

A voice called to her but she saw no one. Willow propped herself up to peer over the counter. "Hello, Mayor. How can I help you?" she asked, putting down the small box and coming around to the front of the oak desk.

"I wanted to thank you for the story hour you ran today. The girls came home excited to tell me about it and then something wonderful happened. They spoke about their mother. I've been trying to get them to open up, but they didn't want to talk about it at all, like she hadn't existed. All I wanted to do was talk about her, but I knew I needed to let them grieve as they wanted to. It was so nice to remember the time that she was here, and for just a moment it felt like she was close enough to walk through the door."

Willow listened and let him continue talking without interruption.

"It was really nice."

Willow's throat felt tight as she listened. Her eyes burned with hot tears. At times, there was so much sadness and injustice in the world, and she always absorbed others' pain as if it were her own. She knew exactly what the girls were going through, having lost her own mother. She'd give anything to take away their anguish! But there is beauty in grieving, too, because it's a visceral sensation of how strong our love was.

"So I just came here to say thank you and let you know you are very much appreciated here. If you ever need help with anything, I am indebted to you. Don't hesitate to reach out." He tilted his red hat towards her and then left.

Willow remembered the difficult days after losing her mother. Her breath became shallow. She thought back to when she was little. Her mother had her crawl in her lap, and would say such grandiose words of encouragement: "You'll change the world some day." "You are a glimpse of perfection." Maybe all mothers say it, but it didn't erase the sting of knowing that in her mother's absence, she was failing all her expectations.

After the mayor left, Willow allowed herself to lie on the couch and cry. When her tears dried, she sat up. "Just be good at today," she told herself. "Do everything you need to accomplish to consider today a success, and that will be enough." If she could keep telling herself this, day after day, maybe it would become true.

Willow finished putting away the knick-knacks, swept the floor, and then helped Daylin clean the cafe. "Today was a good day," she thought to herself. When she got up to her apartment, she checked off another day on her calendar. "When I get home, I will try to make my mother proud," she promised herself as she gazed upward.

DAY 5

With an easy start to the day, Willow began to pull out books and leaf through them. Some of the books looked hand-written and had to have been hundreds of years old. Though she was no reader, there was something fascinating about the relationship between a reader and a writer. How someone far away in both time and place could put their thoughts on a page, hours upon hours of imagination enclosed between covers, waiting for you at some other time and place to open the book and get a glimpse into everything they saw and felt for one moment in time. It might be the most intimate relationship possible.

She also appreciated the smell of crisp, old books and how leather became so soft with age. She inhaled the musty smell and it took her back to a memory of when she was little. Aunt Tilly would read to her while her mother worked long and late hours at the hospital. She recalled snuggling in her lap, listening to stories of magical creatures, of a place where the trees were covered in moss and the sky was the deepest blue you'd ever see.

"Tell me more," a little Willow would say, slowly dozing off.

"Well, in this beautiful place there are dragons and fairies…"

"How lovely!" she'd say with a yawn as she huddled under her blanket with her well-loved teddy bear. The thought suddenly occurred to Willow that those had not just been stories, but were tales from Tilly's everyday life here.

Pulling her out of the warmth of a good childhood memory, there was a knock at the wooden door. "Come in!" Willow yelled as she tried to shelve a stack of Elfish mystery novels. The knock came again. Willow walked to the door and there stood a small dragon. His scales were the same sapphire as the sky and Willow stood silently, mesmerized by his beauty. She caught herself staring and corrected course.

"I'm sorry. Do come in. Can I help you find something?"

The dragon hung his head. "I can't come in. Wooden structures and dragons don't mix, I'm afraid."

"Don't be silly, everyone is welcome here. Come in." The dragon hesitated and then followed her into the shop. She inquired, "What are you looking for?"

"I'd love a book about human history."

Willow guided him to the section and pulled out a few choices.

"That's the one!" he huffed excitedly, a small puff of fire escaping his mouth which somehow ignited the entire sports romance section. The dragon's deep green eyes flashed open in embarrassment as he watched the section reduce to a pile of gray ash with flecks of blazing orange.

Willow quickly stomped on it to extinguish the smoldering embers.

"I told you I couldn't come in here," he wailed as his shoulders slagged.

Willow smiled at him kindly and lifted his snout, still warm to the touch, so he was looking at her. "Do you know what a favor you've done for me? I haven't had a single sports romance purchase since I moved here and was about to ship them back! Now I don't have to. What a relief!"

Immediately, his posture changed. "Really? Can I help with anything else?"

"Well… No! No. Not at the moment," she said quickly, hoping he wouldn't burn any other books.

She took his book up to the register and he slowly followed behind her, watching his every step to ensure he wouldn't ignite any other part of the store.

"Say, do you think you could help me each morning? I've been meaning to hire someone to help out and light the fireplace daily, and perhaps you could also help with some of the desserts we are tinkering around with!"

"I don't think that's such a good idea," he replied with a hint of sadness.

"Well I happen to think it is a great idea! Can you be here at eight tomorrow morning?"

"Well…okay," he finally agreed, his tail held just slightly higher as he walked out.

Faeble peered over at Willow. A slight smirk danced on her lips.

"What?" Willow asked her.

"I like the way you handled that."

Willow was surprised for a moment. Living in the city alone, without a job, she didn't really have many opportunities for compliments, and she found that it gave her a warm feeling.

"Thank you," she replied softly.

"I think I'm going to go for a walk, explore the town a bit. Would you like to join me?"

Faeble continued to work in her book. "Sorry, I'm a bit swamped."

Willow walked out of the shop alone. The fresh air, the perfect temperature, it made her feel as if she were glowing from the inside. She walked along the main road, eager to finally see what the town had to offer.

She passed a craft store and then a small park. As she got to the edge of the small park, she could smell something earthy. She let the scent guide her until she arrived at a small tea shop. Willow opened the door and saw no one.

"Hello?" she called out, starting to worry that she shouldn't be there. Along the wall, there were jars of different teas in glass containers with handwritten labels. While she felt it was time to leave, there was an apple tea that caught her eye.

"Hello!" came two booming voices. She looked up to see two looming figures, ogres, she was pretty sure.

She couldn't hide the quiver in her voice, "Hello… I was just…looking." Willow suddenly felt very small.

"Who are ya?" the man said abruptly. "Never seen ya around." She glared at his arms which were thick as car tires.

"I'm…" she paused, almost forgetting her own name. She looked around to see if she could easily make her way out. "Willow. I'm helping run the bookshop."

"Ah, I'm Ogle…and that there is Thorpe." Thorpe just grunted in reply.

"Would you like to sample our newest tea?"

And something about the innocence of that question, made her put her guard down just a bit. "Sure," she said tentatively.

The large creature moved around the shop, collecting a small and beautiful teacup with matching saucer, scooping dried tea leaves into a strainer, and then pouring hot water into the strainer. He tipped over an hour glass to set the timer. His large frame mingling with such dainty things was such an interesting juxtaposition that she couldn't help but stare. When he was done, he looked up. "Would you like milk and sugar?"

She cleared her throat. "Yes, one sugar please. No milk. Thank you."

There was one small table in the front of the shop where she sat down and waited for the timer to tell her that her tea was ready. When it was, Willow stirred the tea with caution, trying to release some of the pent up heat so she could enjoy it at the perfect temperature. As she did so, it also released the aroma—it smelled like all the good things about autumn. When she took her first sip, the taste was warm and inviting— notes of nutmeg, apple, and a hint of vanilla. It tasted like an apple pie in a cup.

"This is delicious!"

And both Ogle and Thorpe looked pleased.

As she continued to sip, she started to hatch a plan. When she finished, she brought the teacup and saucer to the counter.

"Say, it'd be great if we could team up. We could carry some of your teas in the cafe at the bookshop, and maybe you could have a few books on display here."

Ogle and Thorpe looked at each other. "Yup, we'd like that," said Thorpe. And so over another cup of tea, they hashed out the details.

Back at the shop, Willow told Daylin of her plan. He loved the idea and said he'd work on drafting up a tea menu. She felt a surge of pride—she was going to leave the bookshop in good shape for the permanent owner.

It had been a busy but productive day so far. Willow went to join Faeble on the couch for a moment to rest. The two ladies looked up when they heard a commotion just outside the shop. Willow peered out the front window to see Heilo running. Trailing behind him was a white unicorn, her mane and tail a vibrant pink. The unicorn was gaining on him and was very close to having her horn poke his back.

Willow dashed outside. "Stop!" she yelled. Both turned to look at her. "What is happening here?!"

"I told him to stop swimming in my lake during the morning."

"Surely you two can share a lake."

"We could if he didn't freeze everything he came in contact with!"

Heilo wore a scowl. "It's not like I can help it."

"Let's go inside and talk about this." And the two followed behind her.

They sat at a table and Daylin put a warm cup of coffee before each of them.

"Let's come up with a schedule that works for everyone."

"I'll swim first," bellowed Heilo.

"No, you fool. The lake stays frozen for hours after you leave."

Heilo took a sip of the coffee and the rim lined with frost. Daylin then brought out fresh cinnamon rolls, which seemed to make everyone more amenable.

"Fine, I'll go later in the day," Heilo said, taking the last bite of his food and then licking the plate. "But before lunch!"

Willow looked to the unicorn who rolled her eyes but nodded in agreement. She couldn't help but smile at the majestic creature. Willow was so intrigued by the unicorn that she hoped she'd run into her again soon.

By the time they hashed out all the details, it was time to close the shop. Willow said good night to Faeble and Daylin. Today was rather productive, she thought. Not only had she set up a collaboration with another small business nearby, but she also mediated a conflict. The small voice in her head which normally was so critical said quietly, "I'm proud of myself." She was looking forward to her next day, and forgot to check the current one off on her calendar before climbing into bed.

DAY 6

The next morning, Willow opened the shop at nine sharp. Shortly after, Faeble walked in and resumed her usual spot without purchasing a thing. Willow wondered why she did this each day and what she was working on.

Following behind her was Thorpe, who was holding two large cardboard boxes. "Gotcha yer tea here," he said. Willow pointed him toward the cafe where Daylin greeted him. The two chatted away about the types of teas and set up the display. Daylin called Willow over. The three all shared a cup of tea. This one was lavender, again with a touch of vanilla. It was like comfort in a cup. It was the type of tea that should be drunk with shortbread and a good book. Roaring fireplace optional.

Daylin pulled out his tea menu. It was a sage green with brown writing. The corners were adorned with small birds. Willow scanned the menu.

"It's perfect," she said, looking up to notice they had been staring at her. Willow raised her teacup, "Cheers to a new partnership!" And they clinked their cups to hers.

A knock at the door caused her to excuse herself from the tea party. The dragon appeared at the door.

"Embery, I told you that you don't need to knock."

He looked down at his feet. "Force of habit."

His scales glistened in the sun and before she could stop herself, words tumbled out of her mouth. "You are the most beautiful thing I've ever seen." His eyes widened, they were emerald in color with flecks of gold. He went to open his mouth, but had no words. After an awkward silence, the dragon shuffled past her.

"Right, so let's get you started. First, I'll need you to go over to the fireplace and light it, if you please."

He went straight to his task and Willow made her way over to Faeble.

"That was awkward wasn't it?"

"What?"

"I gawked at him and told him he was beautiful! I just feel like I stick out like a sore thumb here and just don't know how to interact with anyone."

Faeble drew her head back in surprise. "You are understanding it all wrong. Sit down." Willow did as she was told, sinking into the chair. "Embery has been cast aside by all the other dragons due to his size. If you haven't noticed, he is the only dragon in town. I think your compliment took him by surprise—but in a good way."

"I hadn't noticed. I haven't gotten out much actually."

"Well we should change that," said Faeble with a smile.

Once he was done, he came over to Willow and Faeble.

"What's next?"

Willow brought him over to Daylin as Thorpe was excusing himself. She turned to the small dragon. "This is Daylin, our pastry chef extraordinaire. I've had some ideas of new pastries I'd like to add to the shop."

Daylin scuffed his hoof along the ground.

"What's wrong?" asked Willow.

"Nothing," he muttered.

"Clearly you are a bit upset."

"I'm sorry but I am perfectly able to handle the shop on my own. If you weren't happy with the way I was running things you could have talked to me first before bringing in a… a baby dragon!"

Embery spat out a burst of flame and it ignited Daylin's tail. Willow frantically started filling a bucket with water, but as she turned around, the fire was out. She looked over at Faeble whom she saw inserting a wand back into her bag. Willow mouthed, "Thank you!" to her. Her friend gave her a quick wink and then returned to sketching as if she hadn't just saved the whole store and her baker.

"Embery, I like you very, very much, but I can't have you using your fire like that. Now if the two of you weren't so busy acting like stubborn children, you would have let me finish my thoughts." Willow pulled out a small sketchpad from her satchel. She leafed through until she found the hand drawn image to show them. "I'd like you to try to make crème brûlée and meringue pie! Daylin will prepare them and Embery will use his flame to add the finishing touches."

The centaur looked at the dragon and they both nodded in agreement. "Fine, we can give it a try," Daylin responded, somewhat reluctantly. Willow clapped her hands in triumph.

Faeble packed up her satchel and approached Willow at the oak counter. "Do you see it, Willow? See what a good job you are doing so far. And if you can make it one week, you could make it two. And on and on. No matter if it is this, or something else."

Out of habit, Willow was about to say something self-deprecating but then she quashed that nagging voice in her head. "Yes, I did do a good job so far." It sounded strange to hear, but it was true, and she wanted to sit with that feeling for a while.

"Are you a therapist or counselor? You always know the right things to say."

"I am not. Just being a good friend," Faeble said.

"You are a very good friend," Willow replied, and felt her whole body warm.

Willow spent the remainder of the day helping customers and stocking shelves. All the while a little voice in the back of her head said, "I've made a friend!"

DAY 7

Embery showed up eager to work. Daylin, with his generally good-natured attitude, seemed to have put the fire-breathing incident behind him, despite the fact that his tail was still singed at the end. The two started grabbing supplies and from the front counter Willow kept hearing, "Ouch!" "Sorry!" "Excuse me!" She went over to investigate.

"Everything alright here?"

"It's tight quarters boss. If you'd like to expand the menu and double your staff, you might want to consider adding an extension."

Willow shuffled her foot. "About that…you do know I am only here for two weeks, one more at this point. You'll have to ask the next owner, but it seems like a good idea!"

Willow noticed the dragon and centaur exchanging glances.

"…What?"

"Nothing!" They both said very quickly.

She gave them the side eye, holding it for a while to see if they'd crack. Willow moved around the cafe, making her coffee and grabbing a warm buttery croissant. She kept looking back at the two, feeling like they were conspiring about something.

"Morning," Faeble said, walking in and settling in her usual spot. It was the first time she had made her presence known. Willow went over to greet her but she pulled out her notepad and was immersed in whatever it was that she was doing.

Willow began to wander the rooms yet again, still totally unfamiliar with where things were. As she walked, she let her fingers graze the spines, pausing when something caught her interest. She stopped at a book titled, *An Unfulfilled Life*. A wave of sadness came over her. She had one more week before she was supposed to go back to her apartment in NYC, a place where she had no job, no companion, no friends. Willow wondered if she was meant to find this book. She stared at the book on the shelf, waiting for it to rattle or move towards her. It didn't move an inch.

There were no more customers that day so she spent her afternoon opening books and closing them a page or two later. Nothing could hold her attention. She wondered if any book here would be able to captivate her like the stories her aunt used to tell. One thing she knew, she was willing to give it a try now.

As she continued on, she kept hearing a rattling sound and turned corner after corner in search of it. When she arrived at the source, a book with a deep burgundy cover jutted out just a bit. She cupped her hands, and the book leapt down. She turned it to look at the cover. The story was about a lost girl who finds friendship through a community garden. "Pft, no thanks. I'm not one for sappy stories." As she said this the pages literally drooped, expressing their displeasure with her dismissal.

Willow tried to put the book back on the shelf but it kept popping out. "I am not wrestling with a book!" she said with a forceful shove into its original spot. The book leapt out again.

"Fine, if you want to be stubborn, I'm leaving you here on the floor!" Willow looked around to see if anyone had heard that she was now talking to books. The embarrassment subsided when she realized it was just her and this obnoxious book. She walked away, and the book followed, bopping up and down.

She turned on her heels and crouched down to the book. "You sure are persistent for a sappy book!" The book turned itself, showing her its back side in defiance. Willow continued on until she reached the front counter. She tried to organize the receipts from yesterday but the book kept nudging her leg, like a cat trying to persuade its owner for food.

A battle between the book and the unwilling reader ensued. Willow shook her leg to get the book away. It would be thrown off only to return a minute later. It continued to rub up against her leg. Willow looked up when she heard stifled laughter.

"I'm glad you find this funny, Faeble," Willow said.

Faeble, having been caught, let her laughter roll from her like a stream.

"Once you are done cracking up over there," Willow said, shaking her leg again and sending the book flying, "would you please use your magic to help me?"

She had never seen Faeble smile like this before, normally so serious and consumed with what she was working on. "I'm afraid that's not possible."

"You told me anything is possible."

"I did. But that book won't be able to give you up no matter how hard you try to get rid of it. It's decided that it's meant to be read by you. That book will change something within you."

Willow scoffed. "Highly doubt that. This book looks like it's for girls who wear pink bows in their hair and skip around town...not that there is anything wrong with that, but it certainly isn't my style."

"Maybe that is true, but if you don't read it, you're going to have that book follow you everywhere until you do."

Willow rolled her eyes and said to the book, "Fine, I'll read you tonight if you let me be while I finish working." The book felt satisfied with this and perched itself on the counter, waiting for her to keep her end of the deal.

Willow walked over to the young adult section, which had been made very disorganized by a group of witches and wizards. She took out all the books and sorted them—alphabetically by author's last name. There was something about this that she found comforting, the monotony and simplicity of it. It took her several hours to sort it all, but she felt so calm afterwards. Maybe a bookshop wasn't such a bad place to spend her time.

When Willow climbed the steps to her apartment, she heard a soft thud with each step she took. She turned around to see that the book had followed.

Pouring tea leaves into a strainer, she made a cup of tea that smelled of jasmine. Then she cracked the book open, mostly so it would stop acting like the least endearing pet possible. Several paragraphs in, Willow's mind began to slowly slip from this world and deeper and deeper into the world the words created for her. In between chapters she took long sips of her tea, thinking about what she had just read. Letting the words sit with her for a moment. One sentence caught her attention. The beauty of the words took her by surprise. How could a combination of words on paper make you feel so strongly? She rolled the phrase around on her tongue a few times, not willing to let it go.

The deeper she got into the story, she felt like she was walking alongside the characters, starting to feel their ups and downs as if they were her own. She read until her eyes became heavy. She fell asleep, the open book over her chest, her only blanket for the night.

DAY 8

There was a knock on her door, not to the shop but to her apartment. "Oh no!" she shouted, realizing she overslept.

"Ms. Willow, are you alright?"

"Yes, yes! I'll be right down." She removed the burgundy book from her chest. She was four chapters in and had fallen asleep while reading last night. Willow rubbed the sleep from her eyes, having gotten only a few hours of rest.

She quickly threw on a jean skirt and dark purple top, then closed the door behind her so she could go meet Daylin in the cafe. As she descended the stairs, she was buttoning her aubergine cardigan. In the cafe, he already had a latte and scone waiting for her.

"I'm so sorry I overslept," she apologized.

The book hopped up onto the table next to her.

Willow took a large bite of the scone and exclaimed, "What is this? Other than a little slice of heaven!"

Daylin smiled, "I thought you'd like it. It's made from Elixberry, which only grows here in Sapphire Forest. They have to be hand-picked at midnight before the petals close around the berry."

"You can't just peel the petals back? So that you can go at a more reasonable hour?"

"You could, but you wouldn't have a hand anymore."

Willow drew back from surprise.

He shrugged. "Some things are only nice at certain times of the day. Like humans, how they need their coffee first."

She chuckled and then took her next bite. "It's so flavorful and sweet! You picked these last night…at midnight?"

He looked down at his hooves, "Yes, ma'am." She got up and hugged him. "It's really no problem. I like keeping my hands. I'm quite fond of them."

"You were working at midnight! You really didn't have to."

"I had insomnia and was wandering the forest anyway. But I am glad you like it. Try the latte. I extracted some of the juice from the berry and made a simple syrup with it. The latte is Mocha and Elixberry."

Willow brought the mug to her lips and didn't speak for several beats, letting the wonderful combination linger on her tongue.

"Perfection!"

"I added an extra espresso shot, since it isn't like you to oversleep. I thought you could use it."

"You are too good to me," she said.

He smiled at her sheepishly and went back to the kitchen.

As she continued to eat and drink, the book started to rumble on the table. "Oh, no no no, we are just getting to the good part and I'm afraid I'll get too entwined in the drama. We will have to wait until the store is closed." The book rumbled again. "Yes, I realize there are no customers here." It tilted itself backward and fell back dramatically onto the table.

Embery piped up from the kitchen, "Will you just read the book! I can't take anymore of this one-sided conversation."

Willow picked up the book and walked to the front. She propped her elbows on the counter and said, "Just a few minutes."

Hours went by before the bell chimed with a customer. She looked up to see Faeble entering. "Good morning!"

"Morning? It's 2pm. Ohhhh, I see. You've found the one."

Willow laughed. "I had always hoped 'The One' would be a tall, dark, and handsome man. Just my luck it is a book. But yes, I'm enjoying it."

The young wizard from a few days earlier came in. "Hello! How are the school books working out?"

"Fine, I guess," he said solemnly. He looked like a wilting flower.

"Did you need another book for school or something to read for fun?"

Santiv drew closer and Willow sensed he was embarrassed about something. His voice was light like the morning dew. "Do you have any books…about making friends?"

It occurred to Willow this was what felt so familiar about this boy when she first met him. They were the ones who floated through life alone, always looking over their shoulder for someone to talk with or someone to notice them.

"I actually have that exact book coming in tomorrow. Could you come back tomorrow after school?"

"Um, yeah, I guess." He started to turn away.

"But wait! If you're free now, I need help in the kitchen!"

"You do?" said Daylin from behind the cafe counter.

"Yes, Daylin!" she said kindly but forcefully. "Weren't you just talking about how you could use some extra help around the time kids get out from school?" Her eyes grew wide and he caught what she was saying.

"Yes, boss! I was just saying how we definitely need extra help. Would you be interested in working in the cafe after school?"

"Yes!" Santiv said enthusiastically.

"Great!" said Willow. "Daylin will show you around now."

After the boy got a tour, he left, holding himself a little bit higher.

"Do you have a shipment coming tomorrow?" Faeble asked.

"No, I don't think so. Now that I think of it, I actually don't even know how to order books or find out when they are coming." That familiar feeling was returning—out of her element, not being able to accomplish the things that needed to be done.

"So what is your plan?"

"My actual plan? I have none. But I have all night to figure it out."

Willow thought for a while about how she could boost this boy's confidence. She hoped whatever she came up with didn't end up backfiring. Was she, awkward herself and completely out of touch with this world, able to help someone like Santiv to magically become popular?

Frustrated that she interjected herself into this situation without a plan, she closed the shop and headed upstairs to read. As she read, the main character was just beginning to come out of her shell when she reconnected with a childhood friend. Willow placed a blue strand of yarn in the book and closed it, pausing to think. The passages gave her an idea and she started to develop a plan.

DAY 9

Willow entered the cafe, which today smelled of vanilla with a touch of cinnamon.

"Less than a week until it's time for me to go back home," she said aloud. But Daylin and Embery continued to work without responding. "Did you hear me?" she said louder this time.

"Hmmm mmm." they both replied, and went about bustling through the kitchen to prepare for the day.

She felt an emptiness from the interaction. An attachment to the people and town was starting to form and she had hoped they would feel the same. She wanted them to say something like, "Please come back and visit us!" "Don't forget us, Willow!" But no such reaction. Maybe she was just as lost here as in the big city.

She left the cafe and wandered around the store, lost in thought. Maybe she was being unreasonable to expect that people would become attached in such a short time. But she was sure she felt a connection to the people she had spent the past week working with. It would be nice if they felt the same. She felt her eyes line with tears and then told herself, "No, we are not doing this. Not here. Not now."

The front bell chimed, and a large shipment of books came in through the door. There were boxes upon boxes, and she knew it would take her a long time to put them all away. It gave her something to focus on that pulled her out of self-pity.

"Well I guess I know what I'm doing all morning," she said to Faeble.

"I can help," her friend replied. Faeble cast a spell to sort them into genres but Willow asked to put them away herself, to better learn the layout of the store. Over a week in and she still hadn't fully figured this place out!

None of the new books were about friendship and she knew Santiv was coming in soon. But that was ok because she had figured out how to help this boy with his quest to fit in. Willow picked up her phone and dialed the mayor.

His warm voice came through the receiver, "Hello, Willow! How can I help you?"

"I need a big favor! Can you please reach out to the school and tell them that we will be having an event in the cafe? Free coffee and desserts for all students."

"After how kind you've been to my girls, I'd do absolutely anything you asked…as long as it got council approval of course. I'll make the call right away."

"Thank you!" She hung up the phone and got back to putting away the new shipment.

Willow walked with a large stack of books, winding left and right, right and left. "Faeble," she called up to the front. "A little help here! I think I'm lost." She looked down to see a sparkling line leading the way. When the line stopped, she searched the titles and indeed it had brought her exactly to where she needed to be. After shelving the books, she followed the line guiding her back to the front counter.

With that task finished, she sat across from Faeble. "Are you my guardian angel?"

Faeble looked at her in shock. "I am a fairy! Not an angel!"

"It's just a term…like for someone who guides you through everything."

"Hmph, I still don't like it."

"Well, I'm trying to say thank you. I don't know how I would have gotten through this week without your help."

"Sometimes we need a little guidance to see that in fact we can do anything on our own." Willow shrugged. Fae continued, "You are capable of anything and everything, Willow. You just need to be open to succeeding."

Faeble started to turn back to her journal but Willow stopped her. "What are you working on?"

"Just working in my notebook."

"Well, I see that."

"Then why did you ask?" Faeble then pulled out her fountain pen and buried her head in her journal. Willow normally would have been offended by such a remark, but she was starting to get used to Faeble's matter-of-fact speaking.

"Well, I guess I'll leave you to it. I have to get Santiv set up in the cafe."

"I think that will be good for him," her friend replied, still looking at the journal.

Daylin and Embery had worked extra hard to prepare for the influx of expected customers. The whole store smelled of espresso, sweet milk, and baked chocolate chip cookies. Warmth radiated from the cafe since the oven had been going full force all day.

The young wizard came in and went straight back to the kitchen. He tossed on a tan apron which just read, "Cafe". As interesting and creative as her aunt had been, she sure didn't have a knack for naming things. Daylin handed him a name tag and he used a marker to scribble his name. Willow looked on, seeing what she thought might be pride written on his face as he did so.

Daylin put him behind the counter and soon a slew of young witches and wizards were lined up for their lattes and treats. From the counter she could hear, "Wow! You work here? That's so cool."

"Can you make everything on the menu?"

"What's it like to work in a cafe?"

"I wish my mom would let me get a job after school so I could have my own spending money!"

Once the cafe was sufficiently packed, Willow walked up to Santiv. She leaned down, "Why don't you call it a day and sit down with some of your classmates?"

He took off his apron, looking apprehensive. Just then a group of girls called him over to settle a dispute of how Americanos were made and whether or not they were actually invented in America. Willow smiled knowing that the young boy just needed a chance to feel comfortable and then he would be able to open up.

It warmed her heart to see Santiv chatting with his classmates, but the buzz of so many people talking in a small space started to feel overwhelming. She could feel anxiety rising up in her. Her book hopped over to her and rubbed her leg. "I'll be ok," she said, and it went back to the counter.

She felt like she was standing on a cliff: she could either calm her nerves and talk herself off the ledge, or succumb to the oncoming panic attack and fall straight into the abyss. "Going out!" She yelled over her shoulder.

Willow didn't even look to see if she was acknowledged. Her mind raced, throwing attack after attack at her like stones in a glass house, and she could feel her walls starting to crack. She walked along the cobblestone, trying to focus on her five senses to bring down her trembling. She closed her eyes and took in a deep breath. The sensation of being hugged made her open her eyes. As she did so, she realized she was above the ground. The moss from the trees wrapped itself around her and was moving her slowly up. She didn't know where it was taking her but she had no fear.

Gently, like a leaf in the wind, she moved from the ground

to the top of the tree. Perched up high, she could see the stars and the deep sapphire sky. It was incredibly quiet. Then she heard a soft rustling as Faeble flew through the leaf-covered branches.

"I saw you run out. I just came to see you were okay," whispered Faeble.

"I am now," Willow replied as she reached for her hand, and they looked at each other and smiled. Without another word, they basked in the stillness of the night for a moment that stretched on and on.

"We better get back," Willow finally said. Her muscles had relaxed, her heart rate and breathing had regulated. She was going to be okay. Still holding her hand, Faeble stretched her purple wings and they flew from the trees to the lush, moss-covered ground.

The two women walked toward the bookshop. Willow blurted out, "Faeble." And her friend turned to look at her. "You…" Faeble watched her, waiting for her to continue. "You soften my rough edges."

Faeble closed her eyes for a moment and nodded, eyes still closed. When she opened them she smiled at Willow. "And you see that I have any definition at all, Willow."

"What do you mean?"

"I keep to myself and most people are content to let it stay that way. But you always reach out, ask what I'm doing. It's nice to be noticed."

Then she entered the shop, with Willow in tow. They realized it was getting rather late. When it was time to close the shop, Santiv walked up to her.

"Thanks for…everything."

"Will I see you tomorrow?"

"Actually, can I have tomorrow off? They invited me to a game after school!"

"Absolutely!" Her plan had worked!

Once she shut off the lights to the shop, she eagerly

reunited with her book. Like a kitten, she crawled up into the corner of the couch. She placed a mug of hot earl grey tea that Ogle had gifted her on the side table. Then she wrapped a chunky knitted blanket over her lap. As soon as she cracked open the book, she let her mind disconnect from the world around her and into the author's world until sleep consumed her.

DAY 10

Willow sat at the counter waiting for her first customer. When none came, she cracked open her book again and continued to read. Its pages were soft, and with each page turn she felt less in a bookshop and more in the world that the words created for her.

She was so immersed in the words that she forgot where she was, when it was. Willow closed the book and then her eyes, absorbing every last minute in that world. Then she twirled around, clutching the book.

"You alright over there," came Embery's voice from the cafe.

Willow felt a twinge of embarrassment, having totally forgotten that anyone else was here. She carried the book with her to the cafe. "I think I just fell in love."

Daylin peered around the corner, looking shocked.

"This book is just the most beautiful thing ever written!"

His eyes flashed understanding and he went back to his food prep.

"Can you think of anything more powerful than the connection between a reader and a writer? Someone could be far away in distance and time, typing away hours and hours of thoughts…and then that gets into *your* hands and into your mind! It's as if you become one with this complete stranger."

"So are you a reader now," Daylin called from the kitchen.

"Well, I'm going to let myself savor this one a bit longer. And then we shall see." She turned to Embery. "How are the crème brûlées coming along?"

Before Embery could answer, a cackle came from the kitchen.

"Sorry! Sorry! But you just have to come see our attempts."

Willow followed the sound of Daylin's voice to find three or four dozen white ramekins—all with completely scorched custard. Embery rolled his eyes. "I'm glad you find this funny."

"They say practice makes perfect. So…let's keep at it!"

She pulled Daylin aside. "This isn't going to break the cafe's budget is it?"

"Nah, I suspected there would be a bit of trial and error so I got some of the ingredients in town that they were about to toss. Figured we'd do a test run on nearly expired stuff first."

"Smart!" She went to give him a high five and then felt self-conscious. She awkwardly pulled back her hand and ran it through her hair. Daylin smiled at her and they stared at each other, holding the gaze for a moment too long, as if they both wanted to say something but didn't.

Through the front window, Willow noticed something that caught her eye. "Daylin! I'll be right back," she called towards the kitchen. "Do you mind watching the front counter for me?" Once she got his reply, she opened the heavy door and walked outside. The air was warm and inviting. It smelled of sweet lilac.

Willow had seen the unicorn again, and instinctively followed. The majestic creature was now trotting away into the Sapphire Forest—but she was wailing. Something was definitely not okay, and Willow now felt compelled to see if the unicorn needed help. Though Willow said she would only be gone a minute, she continued to follow along a lengthy, cobblestone path. At last she saw the unicorn with a young foal. Willow hid behind a tree, evaluating the exchange. Her eyes went to the small creature and noticed it was hurt. The unicorn looked distressed as it paced back and forth trying to take care of the foal.

Willow quietly tip-toed back until she was out of earshot. Then she picked up her pace and ran back to the bookshop. She threw open the door and breathlessly managed to get out, "Daylin… Go to the forest, young foal…hurt!"

"Where?"

"Straight down the path." She watched him gallop off at top speed, leaving her in the shop to wait and worry.

Thump, thump, thump. Willow tapped her fingers on the counter impatiently, waiting for Daylin to return and give her an update. Two hours had passed. When the door opened, she looked up so quickly she could have gotten whiplash. "Is everything ok?" She blurted out.

"Yes," he responded, though his voice still held some sadness.

"What's wrong?"

"I'm not exactly sure, but according to the nurse we got him to the vet just in time. He will have a long road ahead for recovery."

"There is no magic to help with that?"

"No, our magic doesn't work like that. We can't bring people back whom we've lost and we can't cure ailments or injuries."

Willow sighed. Daylin approached her.

"Thank you, Willow. Your nosiness probably saved his life."

She wasn't sure if she should laugh or hug him. She decided not to overthink it and did both, throwing her arms around his neck and giggling softly.

"I always knew that trait would come in handy one day."

When the day was over, Willow walked into the cafe and offered to help Daylin clean up. She scrubbed the dishes as he put away ingredients.

"Do you like being here?" he asked, cutting into the quiet.

"Of course. Everyone here is so kind. How about you?"

"Well I don't really have a choice. Centaurs only live in the Sapphire Forest."

"What about everyone else?" she asked, picking up another plate to scrub.

"Most people have some other options, but they like it here. There is an eclectic mix of magical beings. It keeps life interesting. I imagine people say similar things about New York."

Willow laughed, "Yes, life is definitely interesting there."

"But do you like it there?"

She thought for a moment. New York had always been her home, but she had a taste of a different life here. "New York is everything all at once. It's silent mornings and bustling evenings. There are people decked out in luxury clothes passing by people who can't afford their next meal. I always thought it was the place for me—it's all these things jumbled together in a way that doesn't make sense, like me. But now I'm not so sure..."

Daylin just nodded his head, not affirming nor contradicting her thoughts. He said nothing, so she was allowed to play the contradictions in her mind, and think of where she fit into it all.

As she thought, she cleaned. She scrubbed the counter with a damp cloth. She mopped the floor as Daylin put away clean dishes. The cafe was sparkling but Willow didn't want to say goodnight to her new friend.

"Would you like to have some tea?"

The two went upstairs. When he entered the living room, he looked around.

"What?" she asked, noticing his curiosity.

"I just thought the place would look different."

"Oh, did you? Like how?"

"More art, more pictures. You seem like the artsy type. But I guess you didn't want to settle in for just two weeks."

"No, this is actually exactly how my apartment looks back at home. It all magically appeared. I guess I've moved around so much that I didn't put much thought into making a home a home."

Daylin approached the coffee table as Willow placed down two cinnamon apple teas. The dried fruit bobbed lazily at the top like tubers in a river. Willow could practically see the wheels turning as he noticed the romance novel sitting on the table. On the cover was a hockey player and a girl in a miniskirt leaning against him.

"I know what you are going to say."

"I'm not going to say anything!"

She noticed he was trying to force down the corners of his lips to hide his smile. "You were going to say that you didn't think this would be a book I'd read."

Daylin gave in and smiled, exposing his bright white teeth.

"Well, I happen to like a book with a good puck," she said confidently. Daylin spit out his tea, spraying it everywhere and then looked absolutely mortified. But Willow was rolled over in laughter. "It's actually a book I was carrying around when Embery lit my entire romance section on fire. It's the sole survivor."

"A survivor amongst books!" Daylin said gallantly.

"And look at the hero's welcome you gave it! Spitting tea all over it." They both chuckled but his cheeks flushed crimson.

Long after the teapot was emptied, they continued to chat. "You are so easy to talk to," she blurted out and then immediately wanted to reel the words back in. "I just mean… It's really, really nice to sit and talk…with you."

Daylin moved a little closer to her, but still gave her some distance. "Same," he said simply.

The calendar hung on the wall, days and days without an "X" counting down her time left in Sapphire Forest.

DAY 11

Willow awoke to the sound of bickering. Maybe pairing up Daylin and Embery wasn't the genius idea she thought it was. She just hoped she'd be able to give Embery a purpose. And the little voice in the back of her head said, "But who will help you find your purpose?" She wanted to say something triumphant like, "I will be the one to find my purpose!" But she didn't believe that, so why lie to herself?

"So we are still at each other's throats?" she asked the two once she was down. They turned around, a wave of guilt taking over their facial expressions.

"Sorry, boss. We were just having some…artistic disagreements," Daylin said.

"You called me a fire-breathing dessert-ruiner."

"Daylin!" Willow scolded, "If you are going to hurl insults, at least they could be more mature than something a toddler would come up with!"

And they all laughed. It broke the tension and the two bakers went back to trying to figure out how to overcome this issue that had left the kitchen covered in burnt desserts and a smoky smell lingering in the air.

"Hmmm… It almost smells like a campfire in here," Faeble said, taking her normal spot.

"Yeah, that's one way to think of it!" remarked Willow.

"There are always multiple ways to think of a situation."

"I know you want to say more to me."

A mischievous look crossed her face, "What do you think I'm trying to say?"

"Well, you were going to say that I could look at my time here as a failure or a success, based on what I focus on."

"I was not! I was going to say some people hate black licorice, but a large portion of Scandinavia loves it. But if that's where your mind took you, then I suggest you explore that further."

"Faeble…did you just make a…joke?"

"I may have."

Willow walked through the bookstore, finally having learned how to get to each section. The overwhelming feeling she had felt from its size was replaced by a new feeling. The large, twisty rooms now felt like a little hideaway. She was on the hunt for a short book, one that she could finish before she had to head back home. She found a poetry book that peaked her interest and pulled it off the shelf. There was artwork inside that she found beautiful and thought this would be the perfect choice.

Willow walked to the front of the store with the book as she heard a few people enter. She greeted each and then sat in the cafe. "What are you reading?" Faeble asked.

"Just a poetry book I found."

"Let me know what you think when you are finished."

The poetry was about different aspects of nature that could be found in the Sapphire Forest. The language was simple but beautiful. Willow liked how each page explored an element of nature with its own poem, like a slow walk through the park.

"You know, I'd rather be in nature than read about it. How about I close the shop and we take a stroll?"

Faeble started putting her journal and pen away, and Willow took this as a yes. They walked along the path, the warm evening creating a blanket around them.

"Can I ask you something?" Willow said, trying to figure out how to say what she had been wondering since her arrival.

"Sure."

"Well, I notice you just hang around the store every day and… Well, I guess I just want to know why."

"Your aunt became a close friend of mine. She noticed I often worked alone on a bench nearby. One day, she invited me to come to her store. She encouraged me to sit and work there so I wouldn't be alone, and I guess I'm just a creature of habit."

"That's really nice," said Willow. Then she thought further, "I can get into habits too, but usually they aren't good ones. I seem to get stuck a lot."

"Do you feel stuck here?"

Willow stopped walking. It took Faeble a few beats to realize and then she stopped, too, turning to look at her friend.

"I don't actually."

Willow's view of this place and her time here had slowly started to change, like autumn leaves changing from green to vibrant sunbursts. She had fully abandoned her countdown calendar. Her thoughts on returning home had morphed from eagerness to apprehension. She wondered what returning to New York City would be like. Would she be able to make herself feel at home in her actual home anymore? Would she be able to try to make some friends like she had here? Most importantly, would she be able to feel the way she did here? More than just *unstuck*—seen, accepted…happy.

"Well, you'll have to come back and visit often," Faeble said to her.

"Yeah…" was all she could say, feeling a burning sensation flash in her throat. There were things she wanted to say, but she let them remain in her thoughts. She'd hold on to them, at least for now.

DAY 12

aylin knocked on Willow's door even before the birds began to chirp at her window.

"Everything okay?" she yelled through the door.

"Yes, but get dressed quickly and come see this!"

Willow followed his directions, tossing on clothes without assessing if they matched or not. After pulling her hair up in a bun, she met him in the kitchen. Embery stood proudly in front of the table. When she entered, he moved to the side, showing the most beautiful desserts, including several crème brûlées and lemon meringues. Willow clapped her hands together. "You did it Embery! See, your fire-breathing is an asset, not a liability."

All three had pleased smiles on their faces, and resumed their morning duties. Then, Willow remembered something, and pulled Daylin aside. "Any word on the foal?" she asked with concern.

"Oh yes, sorry I forgot to tell you. He's improving and they think he should be able to leave by the end of the week."

Willow cupped her hands around her mouth. "Oh, thank goodness." she breathed. She realized she wouldn't be there to hear any more updates and she turned away to hide her disappointment.

The bell rang as a customer entered the store, and Willow excused herself. She saw a bright white furry figure and greeted him, "Heilo! How are you?"

He grunted a reply.

"What can I help you with?"

He looked down at his feet but said nothing.

"Come on now, there is no need to be shy."

It took him several grunts before she understood that he was embarrassed. She leaned in and let him whisper in her ear, a slight chill gliding across her skin as he spoke.

"Yes! I have the perfect book for you. Just give me a minute."

Willow ran up to her apartment and grabbed the romance book off the table. She handed it to Heilo and his huge smile took up most of his face. Heilo sat down in the cafe with an iced latte and *So Pucking Good.*

Later, a group of sprites floated in. They flew through the store with the grace of a ballerina and the self-confidence of a CEO. In the kitchen, Embery was blowing fire to finish the crème brûlées. Willow looked around and couldn't help thinking that she didn't really have anything to add to this town. She was just a plain, boring, non-magical being. What good was that to anyone?

One sprite approached her and asked with a voice dripping with confidence, "So where can I find your books covering the Sprite chronicles?"

Willow thought for a moment and glanced around the store, hoping the book would make itself known if they had it. "I'm sorry, I'm afraid I haven't seen that." She noticed the other sprites giggling behind her.

"That's because it doesn't exist. How can you possibly run a magical bookshop with zero magical knowledge?"

Her instinct told her to turn to Faeble, to have her fix the situation like she always did. It amazed her that people like this actually existed, people who used hurting others as a sport.

But Willow decided she could and should handle this on her own, so she stood a little taller before responding, "I'd love to be able to help you find something that fits your needs. Perhaps I can interest you and your friends in our newest arrival?"

"Yah, what's that?" the sprite asked, hands on her hips.

"It's called *Overcoming the Sprite Superiority Complex*. Instant Best Seller."

Faeble, who had just taken a big swig of her iced latte, choked on the cool liquid. The sprites left in a huff as Faeble looked on pleased as pie.

Dealing with rude customers was nothing new to Willow. However, here it hit differently. They were telling her to her face that she didn't belong. The worst part was she knew it was true. That thought hung with her the rest of the day, bringing her mood down.

As stars appeared gold and brilliant in the sapphire sky, Willow closed the store. Defeated, she called out to Faeble. "I'm closing up but you're welcome to stay as long as you'd like…if you'd like to keep working."

"There is actually a midnight festival in town, would you like to join me?"

Willow thought for a second. It sounded like fun, but she'd feel out of place.

Faeble noticed her hesitation. "Something is making you doubt yourself, I can see it in your face."

Willow bit her lip. "I don't fit in here. Everyone has all these amazing skills." The slight sound of footsteps couldn't be heard over her sniffling. But she knew Faeble was behind her before she even felt a hand on her shoulder. Willow turned around as Faeble raised a finger towards her cheek. She lifted the tear from her face, and it lay perched on her finger. A poem between two people—as if she were physically lifting the sadness from her friend and taking it on herself. A shared sadness was easier to bear.

"Don't let those sprites get you down. They are like that with everyone."

"No, they are right. I have nothing to offer this town… maybe any town."

"And you don't have your own skills? Come on."

"I can put books away."

"A very important skill for an owner of a bookshop!"

"Oh please! Look at you, you can fly! You can create magic to do whatever you need." Faeble smiled. "What?" Willow asked.

"You have your own magic."

"I don't and I'd rather not have that on full display at the festival."

"Your magic is in how you make everyone feel. You make people feel included, appreciated, and seen. What *real* good is being able to illuminate the ground to guide people to something? You make people see something good in themselves, make them happy. I can't think of anything more magical than that. Come to the festival and watch. Everyone will be so glad you are there. You deserve to see the magic you created within all of us."

Willow decided to give it a go. She had only two more days here—so what if she felt out of place? She wouldn't see any of these people again. Faeble led her along the cobblestone pathway to a part of town she had never seen. At the end of the street was a setup for a small festival, tents lining the way with townsfolk selling their wares. Each stand was aglow with small, illuminated bulbs.

"Fairy lights?"

"Sure, how do you think they got that name?"

Willow laughed. As she and Faeble visited the tables, Willow felt warmed by each encounter. She knew so many of these people from the shop. There was Heilo who was selling ice cream. The mayor and his daughters had their own stand for his re-election campaign. Santiv was at the table for the school with some other classmates, and laughing easily. Passing each familiar friendly face, the voice in the back of her head softened and said, "This feels like home."

Faeble led her to an empty table. She opened her satchel and began to set up.

"This is your stand?"

"Tonight it is our stand," and she handed her a box to unpack.

"Faeble! What is all this?"

"Artwork."

"I see that but is it your artwork?"

"Yes," she said shyly.

"It's breathtaking," Willow said, admiring a sketch of the forest.

"You are still breathing."

Willow pondered how she could reword her feelings. "When I look at this, it makes me happy. For just a moment, nothing else exists around me and all I can see is what you created. I like the colors and the subject. I love it all." This the fairy understood.

"I'm glad you like my art. Are you still reading that poetry book?"

"I am! The poetry is lovely…but what makes it really special is that it has the most beautiful drawings." Faeble tried to hide her smile.

"Wait a minute…" Willow said, just catching on.

Feeble nodded. "That's my artwork, too."

"Amazing!" Willow looked at the art all around her and was embarrassed that she didn't notice the artistic resemblance sooner. "What are the chances that in all those books, I'd find yours?"

"Statistically very low."

She pulled out a sketchbook and flipped through the pages. "I've been working on something." She turned until she got to a hand-drawn sketch of Willow reading her poetry book behind the counter. "For you," she said. Willow put her hand to her chest as she looked over all the little details. Each book was carefully sketched with a tiny title on the spine. The checkout counter had all the little knickknacks that she had set up. And Willow noticed that she was drawn in her normal get up—long cardigan, mini-skirt, and boots.

"This is the nicest gift anyone has given me. Thank you."

Faeble tore out the drawing and placed it into a small frame. They spent the evening selling artwork, meeting more people in town, and chatting with each other until the sun came up. So this is what it feels like to belong, she thought to herself. She knew she wanted more of it.

Back at home, she was ready for sleep. But first she had something she needed to do. Proudly, Willow took out the framed picture and put it on her wall. She stood back and admired it. It really did feel like home.

DAY 13

After the late night at the festival, it was nearly impossible to wake up on time. When she descended the stairs, Daylin already had her breakfast ready.

"Made you a double espresso! How was the festival last night?"

"It was a lot of fun! Why weren't you there?"

He shrugged. "Embery was feeling anxious so I stayed with him. He was worried he'd get too excited and burn down someone's stand."

"That was so kind of you to do. We have to figure something out to help with that."

"Carry a bucket of water everywhere he goes?"

Willow laughed. "Let's keep brainstorming. So what deliciousness do you have today?" she said as she admired the plate in front of her.

"That is something my mom made for me when I was little, try it!" Willow did as she was told.

The scone had fresh berries encased in a warm vanilla dough. The juice from the berries exploded with each bite and tasted like the first day of summer, vibrant and warm. "Oh Daylin! This is just wonderful."

Today was Willow's last full day in the bookshop, and there was a nagging feeling in the back of her mind but she couldn't place what it was. Something felt—wrong.

There were several customers waiting outside when she went to open the shop. "Good morning!" She greeted them all warmly. A sprite flew above the crowd, too eager to wait her turn in line. Each customer asked for recommendations or locations and Willow provided them what they needed.

A troll approached her and she wanted to comment that she had troll dolls when she was a kid, but then thought better of it. The troll asked what she'd recommend from the cafe. She started talking about the new desserts and noticed that her voice was high-pitched and faster... Was she excited? ... talking about work? This might be the first time she didn't roll her eyes and grunt while explaining some new arrival at her job. The troll went off to the bakery and she could hear him order, "One crème brulee please!"

The same troll approached her with a French cooking book a few hours later. "Thank you for recommending that dessert. My grandmother was French. I don't know if you've ever met a French troll before."

"Can't say I have."

"Well she used to make those. It reminded me how much I miss gathering with my cousins and eating all the amazing treats she'd make."

"And now you are going to try to make them on your own!" she said, admiring how much books could make people feel connected to another time or place. "That's so special. Thank you for sharing that with me."

The troll chuckled, "More likely it will just sit on my coffee table and be a reminder to come back here!"

"That sounds like the perfect plan to me."

"Then I'll see you the next time I get a sweet tooth."

Willow sighed, "I'm afraid tomorrow is my last day. I have to go back to my life in New York City."

"Ah, what awaits you there?"

She paused. "Well…nothing." Her cheeks flushed red and hot with embarrassment. He looked saddened by this but wished her luck before taking the book and walking out of the store.

A melancholy washed over her. What was she going back for? Like, truly for? There was no job, no pet, no family, no companion. She knew she had to go back—her life was there…but was it a life at all?

Santiv walked in with a group of friends. They all sat at the cafe, enjoying lattes and desserts. While she wasn't exactly eavesdropping, she did look over to check on him from time to time. The ease at which he was able to chat with these other kids filled her with pride.

Once everyone was taken care of, she noticed Faeble. Willow wanted to tell her she'd miss her, but she thought Faeble might not be comfortable with an emotional conversation.

"Well, you did it," Faeble said, interrupting her thoughts.

Willow looked around. The customers were taken care of, the bookshop was clean and running well. She had done it.

"I did! And I'm glad I came to help out."

"Back at home, will you work in a bookshop?"

Willow knew her time here would be over in a flash, but wasn't really sure what she would do when she got back home.

"That's an idea. To be honest, I'm not really sure. I don't have a plan right now."

And then that nagging feeling of something not being right materialized itself. "Tell me to stay," her mind whispered to Faeble.

The phone rang and Willow picked it up. "Books," said Willow, lamenting about the name once again. "How can I help you?" Willow nodded. "Hmmm… Ok. Yes… Sure."

She hung up the phone, and Faeble asked, "Who was that?"

"The Realtor. The shop has sold. The new owner will be here tomorrow."

"That's good. I'm working on a new sketch," her friend said to her.

"That's great, Fae. I'm sure it will be amazing. I wish I could see it," she said, a bit distracted. She peered around the shop.

Faeble looked at her seriously. "Well then, you'll have to come back to visit."

She didn't respond. She had been transported here by a car she didn't hire. How would she even be able to return?

The mayor and his girls came into the store, the latter like three tiny hurricanes. They zipped around collecting stacks of books as they moved through the sections. When they approached the counter, they each put their books on top. As Willow was checking them out, she noticed a line forming. It was another 30 minutes before she got through the line.

"Phew," she exclaimed when the line finally died down. As she checked over the sales for the day, she saw that it was the best day the store had since she'd been there. Then she looked through the sales log and realized it was the best day the shop had in years! "What an amazing way to hand over this shop tomorrow," she thought to herself with both a sense of accomplishment and a dash of regret.

Willow settled into the couch in the cafe area, opting for that over going upstairs to her apartment. Though the store had closed, she invited Fae to stay as long as she wished.

Sitting side by side, she felt the warmth of her friend's leg against hers. Willow smiled as she watched Fae continue to sketch. She took it all in. Two short weeks had brought her so much: friendship, the knowledge that she could succeed at something, belonging. It would be difficult to leave, but she must. There was a new owner arriving tomorrow and they would take over the apartment as well. Even if she wanted to stay, she couldn't.

THE FINAL DAY

Willow woke up with a strange feeling, that feeling that rumbles inside you because you forgot something and your mind is begging you to recall it. She descended the steps, with just a small box of her most important things. She knew the remainder of her items in the apartment would pack themselves up and meet her back in New York City. The cafe and bookstore were both empty and she felt her chest constrict.

She had expected every day to start as it had the two weeks before, with each person in their normal spot. She hoped she could have one more time to watch Fae sit down on the couch and sketch, or be greeted by the smell of Daylin's fresh pastries. She had played goodbyes in her mind all last night and now was met with emptiness and silence. The disappointment weighed heavily on her.

Though the shop was perfectly organized, she lingered a bit, adjusting books here and there. She slowly peeked through the bookmarks to make sure nothing was out of place. All was good and she couldn't find anything else to hold her back.

Willow heard the sound that had originally brought her to this place, the soft bells. Willow looked around and saw the car, but no one else. Somehow, even when everything felt so perfect, she was still alone, still making no impact on the world around her. Maybe it was the loneliness, maybe it was the disappointment, but her feet felt heavy with each step as if they were weighed down by sandbags. The car sat there waiting for her, and a line of glittering gold sparkled on the ground, guiding her to the back of the car, where she thought she'd dump some of her things into the trunk.

She walked slowly and deliberately, trying to soak in the last bits of magic before being plopped back into the "real world." Her eyes filled with tears and she let them fall, allowing herself to fully feel the sadness. She took another step, and then the line bent. Willow watched as the line curved away from the car and back towards the shop. She put one foot in front of the other and continued to follow it like goslings to their mother duck.

When she looked up, everyone was there. Daylin, confident and smiling. Embery, shining and sweet. Faeble, beautiful and shy. Ogle and Thorpe, looming over the crowd while wearing frilly floral aprons. The mayor and his three girls, trying to contain their excitement. And someone new, a beautiful scarlet phoenix.

"What is going on?!" she squealed in delight. They all looked at her, smiling, but allowing her the time to come to her own realization. She followed the path to be closer to her friends. Her family.

"The shop was never for sale, was it?"

The three girls giggled loudly as everyone else warmly nodded their heads.

"We tricked you, Willow!"

"You sure did," she said as she bent down with open arms, and they ran to her embrace.

"Your aunt felt that you'd find yourself here, in this shop, in this town. We hope you agree that this is where you belong, here with all of us as the not-so-temporary bookshop owner of Sapphire Forest," said the mayor.

"Please stay," Ruby said, her head nuzzled against Willow's shoulder.

Faeble spoke next. "You are free to follow the path you'd like: to the car back to New York City or here, your home."

Willow released the girls, and noticed that their butterflies had briefly turned full color, because a show of love can make grief disappear for a moment in time.

The phoenix, feathers a deep shade of ruby, approached. "Your aunt asked me to complete the paperwork to transfer this shop to you, if you'd like it that is."

She didn't hesitate. "Yes, I'd like that very much."

"Let's go inside and complete the paperwork then."

They all went inside but Willow lingered a bit longer, looking at her new shop. She looked at the sign. "I think I'm ready to make this bookshop my own." And just like that the wooden sign's carving of "Books" transformed into "Spellbound Stories". It was now her own. "My home," she said as she continued to follow the glowing path toward her future.

ABOUT THE AUTHOR
& THE INSPIRATION FOR THIS BOOK

Amber Leigh Larrain is an author based in NJ. She lives there with her family and dog. In her free time she enjoys reading, running, and traveling. She has written two psychological thrillers, but this is her first cozy fantasy.

This book was inspired by her first visit to Savannah, Georgia. The very first paragraphs of this book were written in the airport on her way to this new destination. She didn't know it yet but it would be one of the most truly magical places she has ever visited. As she continued to write during her time there, it inspired her. So many elements in this book tie back to that experience: the endless rooms of books at E Shaver Booksellers, the coziness and whimsy of coffee at Mirabelle, and sitting in parks with oak trees draped in Spanish moss. It felt more like a dream than a vacation. She hopes these pages can spark the same magic she found in Savannah.

instagram.com/AmberLeighLarrain
tiktok.com/@AmberLeighLarrain

ALSO BY AMBER LEIGH LARRAIN

Blackout Girl

Until Death Does She Part

Everyone I Love Is Dead - Coming March 2026

Sapphire Forest Book 2- Coming October 2026